Birds in the Rain

PRAISE FOR *STORYSHARES*

"One of the brightest innovators and game-changers in the education industry."
– Forbes

"Your success in applying research-validated practices to promote literacy serves as a valuable model for other organizations seeking to create evidence-based literacy programs."

- Library of Congress

"We need powerful social and educational innovation, and Storyshares is breaking new ground. The organization addresses critical problems facing our students and teachers. I am excited about the strategies it brings to the collective work of making sure every student has an equal chance in life."
– Teach For America

"Around the world, this is one of the up-and-coming trailblazers changing the landscape of literacy and education."
- International Literacy Association

"It's the perfect idea. There's really nothing like this. I mean wow, this will be a wonderful experience for young people."   - Andrea Davis Pinkney, Executive Director, Scholastic

"Reading for meaning opens opportunities for a lifetime of learning. Providing emerging readers with engaging texts that are designed to offer both challenges and support for each individual will improve their lives for years to come. Storyshares is a wonderful start."
- David Rose, Co-founder of CAST & UDL

Birds in the Rain

Rachael Mockalis

STORYSHARES

Story Share, Inc.
New York. Boston. Philadelphia

Storyshares
Story Share, Inc.
24 N. Bryn Mawr Avenue #340
Bryn Mawr, PA 19010-3304
www.storyshares.org

Inspiring reading with a new kind of book.

Interest Level: Middle School
Grade Level Equivalent: 4.1

9781642611076

Book design by Storyshares

Printed in the United States of America

Storyshares Presents

1

It was one of those days when the rain just wouldn't stop. It was cold and wet and the only sounds were the downpour and the occasional blasts of thunder. The sun was blotted out just enough so that it wasn't dark enough to be dark, but it also wasn't light enough to be light.

Truly, it was a somber landscape.

But Lucy wasn't running to get out of the rain.

She was just walking along her way, down some old road with cracks woven throughout and weeds lacing the shoulders.

Wasn't she worried about getting wet? No, her clothes and long, black hair were already soaked to the point where the water just rolled off of her in beads. *Wasn't she cold?* Yes, but it was something she could feel that didn't hurt. All she ever heard in her foster home were harsh, scathing words and orders.

"Lucy! Why don't you ever wear anything nice? You're an embarrassment!"

"Lucy! I thought I told you to do the dishes! I don't care what kind of homework you have! DO THE DISHES!"

"Lucy! Why are you so incompetent?!"

Why was she? She didn't know. She didn't know why everyone hated her, but there must have been a reason. Her parents abandoned her and she had been bounced around from home to home as long as she could remember.

She was all alone.

What was she doing? What was so important that she was out on a day like that? Did she have an appointment to keep? Was she planning something?

The simple truth: she was running, no, *walking* away.

She was walking down that old, forgotten road simply so she didn't have to turn around and go back inside. Inside where her demons dwelt. Inside where no one cared. Inside where she was locked up, forgotten about, and no one bothered to care. Just the thought made her green eyes well up with tears.

Maybe she'd get lost. Lost would be nice. That way, she'd never have to go inside. No one would miss her, anyway. Maybe she'd die. While not the preferable option, at least she might get some peace that way. Maybe someone would finally notice her.

What she really wanted was someone who'd listen to her thoughts and feelings and legitimately CARE. Someone who'd let her get her two cents in without interrupting her. Someone who wouldn't put words in her mouth or accuse her of feeling things she didn't feel or thinking things she didn't think.

Her wishing was interrupted suddenly when a voice called out over the rain, "Looking for something?"

She gasped and turned to see the source of the voice.

2

A boy that looked to be about Lucy's age was sitting casually on a boulder with his legs crossed and his back leaning against an adjacent birch tree, which was partially covered with thick vines. The cover of the tree seemed to keep the boulder mostly dry.

The boy himself had fluffy, light blonde hair poking out from under the hood of his rain coat. His eyes were as blue as Lucy's were green, but seemed more... alive, somehow. He was holding an old acoustic guitar, picking at the strings.

"No need to be nervous," he continued when Lucy didn't reply, "Just wondering."

"Yeah," Lucy replied, just realizing it herself, "I guess I am looking for something."

"You look tired. Why don't you sit down?"

"Tired?" She scoffed as she sat down. Some unknown rage bubbled to the surface. "Yeah, I'm tired alright. I'm tired of everyone and everything always... always..."

"Getting in your way?" the boy finished.

She was shocked to find he was right and muttered, "Yeah."

"What's your name?" He sounded so... nice. No one had ever spoken to her so kindly, with such care. No one had ever asked her name so sincerely before.

"Lucy," she replied, dumbstruck, "and you are?"

"Raphael," he answered, reaching one hand over his guitar for her to shake. She took it and he continued, "Pleased to make your acquaintance. Something wrong? Well, besides... everything." He resumed strumming on his guitar, while still maintaining eye contact.

Lucy looked away, "Sorry, I'm just not used to people being so..."

"Cordial?"

"I was going to say friendly, but... yeah."

"Been there, done that, not going back. So, Lucy, what brings you to this unused back-road in the middle of a forest on a day like this?"

"Life." She pulled her knees to her chest and stared at the cracks in the road while she played with her shoe laces. Even those were drenched.

"Yeah, those bad parts of life can really suck." He started playing some simple but soothing song.

Lucy scoffed again and leaned back, supporting herself with her hands, "I've yet to see any of the *good* parts."

Raphael focused on the song for a moment before replying, "You know, there was a point when I'd stopped believing in those good parts, too."

"Who said I stopped believing in the good stuff?" she gathered up her long hair and wrung it out.

"Come on," he laughed, "it's all over your face. Plus, in my experience, people who believe in good stuff don't take hikes in weather like this."

"Alright, then what made you believe again or whatever?"

"I died."

Birds in the Rain

3

Lucy recoiled from shock, nearly slipping off their stone perch. That was *not* what she expected.

She struggled to reply, "You... you what?"

"Relax," he chuckled, "I'm not a ghost or anything, if you believe in that kind of stuff. I got into a stupid fight and got the tar beaten out of me... and then I was shot.

"Anyway, someone called 911 and I ended up in a coma for three days and, the by sunset of day three, I died."

"I saw the light and everything. So I'm laying there, feeling like I'm slipping away as the doctors are trying to revive me and I'm looking up at that light thinking 'It's a shame nothing in life was that beautiful.'"

"Then, like I was slapped in the face by one of those angels, I... I don't know what the word is. Un-died? Anyway, that's what I did."

Despite herself, Lucy laughed at his inability to find the reverse of death. Then asked, "What happened after that?"

"Enough about me, what about you?"

"Ah, no. That's not how I do things," Lucy hadn't been aware that she *had* a way of doing things, "Finish your story, then I'll tell you mine."

"Okay, then. Where was I?"

"Not dead."

"Right. So I had just un-died. I was in the hospital for four more days before my good-for-nothing parents found me. Those nights I couldn't get myself to sleep. This little girl came and talked to me every night. I never got a good look at that girl those nights, it was always so dark.

I'm not sure why, but I told this little girl *everything* I was thinking and feeling. Finally, I told her about how the only good thing I'd ever seen was that light and you know what she said?"

"What?"

"'Sure you have, you just didn't look hard enough.' I realized that she was right. There was good stuff, but I was so caught up with all the bad things I didn't pay attention."

Lucy smiled. Her insides felt warm, hopeful, but it only served to make her skin feel colder.

"You look like you're freezing," Raphael observed accurately. He took off the raincoat he was wearing and handed it to her saying, "Here, no point in you getting anymore soaked than you already are." He handed it to her so casually, as if it wasn't the nicest thing anyone had ever done for Lucy.

Ever.

She took it with a thanks so soft it melted into the rain perfectly.

"It's getting late," Raphael pointed out, "you should head back."

Lucy didn't want to go. She didn't want to leave and never see him again.

In the rain-painted silence, a bird sang out.

"Funny," Raphael said as he stopped strumming on his guitar, "how that bird sings while all the others are silent. Like its calling out even though no one will answer."

Lucy stared out in the direction of the song.

"Raphael," she began.

"Yeah?"

"You... you're not going to leave and forget about me, are you?"

He chuckled, "No, why would I do that?"

"That's what everyone else who ever pretended to care did."

"Well, I'm not everyone. And I'm not pretending. Besides, I still have to hear whatever it is you've got to say."

"But you still think I should go?"

"Not right now, but soon."

"Then when can we talk?"

"Why don't we meet here the next time it rains?" She smiled again. She realized that she smiled more in the past minutes than she had in a long time.

"Alright," she agreed.

4

Later, on her way back to the home, Lucy memorized every landmark so she could find the boulder and birch tree the next time it rained. She figured she'd be safe from Mrs. Dollar's wrath, since the only evidence of her encounter with Raphael was his raincoat (he insisted she could return it when they met again) and it looked like anything else in Lucy's sparse wardrobe.

Mrs. Dollar (a.k.a. Foster Parent Number 11) was a women who cared about appearances and little else. She was in her late forties/early fifties, despite her claim that she was forever thirty-five. She insisted being called

Missus Dollar, despite the fact that her husband had been dead for years and she didn't seem to care for any men, including her late husband.

She ran Dollar's Home For Girls and Lucy assumed her late husband had some kind of money, because she didn't appear to have any job or monetary issues. In fact, she only ever wore the expensive stuff and pretty much let the girls buy whatever they wanted, as long as she approved first. She insisted that all the girls go to her little, white, Methodist church every Sunday in their best clothes (this was a problem because Lucy was raised as a Catholic by Foster Parents Number One). Mrs. Dollar would always flaunt the girls' accomplishments in public and then admonish them for every shortcoming behind close doors.

Mrs. Dollar's appearance very much matched her personality. She had short, blonde hair that was likely not her natural hair color. Her face was constantly plastered with make-up, giving her face the appearance of a porcelain doll. In a creepy way. Her wide, dark eyes didn't help.

What concerned Lucy about Mrs. Dollar at the moment was the fact that she wouldn't exactly be thrilled if she found out that Lucy had met a boy.

Mrs. Dollar forbid dating or even having male friends. She never listened to logic and once locked a girl in the basement for three days because she held hands with a boy at school. Luckily, Mrs. Dollar didn't care much for the girls outside of appearances and often left them to their own devices.

The lights were off as Lucy approached the home, an old victorian house and (to Lucy's knowledge) the biggest house in town.

The house was three stories high, not including the basement. It had towers, windows, and decorations that were kept in pristine condition.

It was painted bright blue with white accents, giving it the feeling of a sky fortress. That was the only thing Lucy liked about the home.

She climbed up the stairs to the wrap-around porch and entered the side-door, into the kitchen. It was dark and the only light was coming from the flickering TV in the adjacent room.

After a careful peek, she stepped out of the kitchen and climbed the stairs that led to the second and third floors. Mrs. Dollar may not care, but if Carolina caught her, the glamour-girl would find some way to use it against her.

Lucy climbed past the second floor without stopping. Carolina's room was on the second floor. She crept down the hall of the third floor and slipped as quietly as she could into one of the tower rooms.

The five beds in the room were arranged in a circle around a rug. The only light in the room came from a jar-like nightlight on nightstand.

As quietly as she could manage, she pulled down the string and the attached ladder and door. She climbed into her attic bedroom.

On her best days, Lucy didn't mind her room but she definitely didn't feel any affection toward the cramped attic. She was barely able to stand up straight in the shortest part of the cone-shaped ceiling. Her bed was more like a military cot and the only furniture she had besides that was a dresser that stood at half her height and perfectly held her few belongings. Sitting on top of it was an oil lamp and a lighter, her only source of light in the room at night.

During the day, light seeped through the small skylight in the roof. If she climbed up on her dresser, she could open the skylight and climb onto the roof.

Mrs. Dollar hated that.

Lucy changed into pajamas, glad she'd have time to shower in the morning. School had let out for summer about a week ago and, while Lucy enjoyed the reprieve from school life, she hated the extra time she had to spend with Mrs. Dollar.

She laid on her cot and clutched Raphael's jacket, a reminder of the good stuff.

Birds in the Rain

5

Before Lucy opened her eyes the next morning, before she was even fully awake, she felt the morning light creep through the skylight and brush against her face. Despite this, she still hoped for rain.

She kept her eyes closed, clutching the raincoat, until she heard a voice from below.

"OW!" Blake's voice carried a string of profanities through the open attic door, followed by, "LUCY! YOU LEFT THE STUPID LADDER DOWN AGAIN!" Lucy quickly shuffled out of bed.

"Sorry!" she called as she peered down the ladder. She didn't want to upset Blake. Blake was the only girl who tolerated Lucy's presence at the home and was probably the only girl Mrs. Dollar hated more than Lucy.

Blake was goth. Or she at least dressed like it. Her wardrobe was filled with black, dark gray, and the occasional splash of purple and red. The only make-up she wore was dark-colored lipstick and eyeliner. Her hair was black, like Lucy's, but unlike Lucy's, it naturally curled into tiny ringlets.

"Sorry," Lucy apologized again as she descended the ladder.

"Don't *apologize*," Blake replied, her blue eyes looking brighter pre-eyeliner, but also full of anger, "Just remember to put the freakin' ladder up next time!"

"Are you okay?" Lucy asked.

"Sheesh, if I weren't okay, I wouldn't be wasting my time talking to you, I'd call an ambulance or whatever. And you need a shower."

"I know."

"Well, go get it before the other girls wake up."

Lucy decided to listen to Blake's advice.

After her shower, Lucy descended the stairs and retrieved a box of cereal and a bowl from the cabinet.

She sat at the counter and shoveled food into her face as fast as she could, acutely aware that at any minute, the other girls would descend, either in their packs or one by one.

Lucy just put her bowl in the dishwasher when the first pack of girls stomped down the stairs, chattering like a bunch of monkeys.

At the head of the pack was Carolina. Carolina always dressed like she was out to make a statement. She was stupidly gorgeous. She probably wore as much makeup as Mrs. Dollar, but she made it work. If it weren't for her evil personality, she probably would've been adopted years ago just for her looks. She had skin the color of coffee with cream and glamorous, coarse hair, and deep brown eyes. But there was always something about her... if you weren't enamored by her beauty, all you saw was ugly heart.

Lucy kept her head down and shuffled to the living room, where she began to look for something to read. Since Mrs. Dollar never touched the endless books, Lucy assumed that it was Mr. Dollar who was a book person.

"Lucy," Carolina's sing-song voice called, "Could you come here for a second?"

All Lucy could think was, b*ad stuff.*

Hesitantly, Lucy walked over to the kitchen.

When she took too long, Carolina crossed the rest of the distance, holding something behind her back. Blake watched from the counter, sipping her coffee.

"Aren't *you* the one who did the grocery shopping last time?" Carolina asked, accusation tinting her otherwise cheerful voice.

"Yeah, why?" Lucy replied. Carolina's pack was snickering.

Carolina pulled a milk jug out from behind her back, "What is this?"

"Milk?"

"What kind of milk?"

Lucy tilted her head to read the label, "Two percent."

"Uh-huh. And, what has less fat in it? Two percent milk or skim milk?"

"...Skim milk?"

"So, why did you get two percent milk?" Carolina unscrewed the milk's cap with flourishing, twisting motions.

"I don't like skim milk?"

"Oh, please," Carolina held the jug over Lucy's head and turned it upside-down, pouring the rest of the contents on Lucy's head.

Carolina threw the jug at Lucy's stunned face and spat, "No one *cares* what *you* like or don't like or *think*!"

Lucy stood there for a moment, awestruck, before she felt a hand on her shoulder.

She flinched and turned to see Blake.

"You go wash up," she ordered, "I'll clean this up."

"Thanks..." Lucy muttered, wondering what was up with Blake's change of attitude. Normally, one had to beg for her help.

6

It didn't rain that day, but it did the next.

Lucy woke up, overjoyed by the faint pitter-patter of rain on her skylight. Lucy shuffled through her dresser for her blue umbrella and grabbed Raphael's raincoat and threw on some clothes and her shoes.

She practically threw the ladder down and climbed down with obvious excitement.

She stopped by the bathroom to brush her teeth, but decided to skip breakfast.

She practically jogged to the door, only stopping when she heard Blake's voice.

"What's the rush?"

"I'm meeting a friend."

Blake looked at her with disbelief, "Today's grocery day. And after the thing yesterday with the milk? Mrs. Dollar's gonna notice if we don't have milk."

"I'll pick it up on my way back," Lucy promised.

Blake examined Lucy for a moment before conceding, "Alright, but don't forget. And don't expect me to cover for you."

Blake had barely finished her sentence before Lucy was out the door.

As she dashed to the boulder, Lucy forced herself to crush her own hopes, telling herself he probably wouldn't be there.

But Raphael was waiting for her, in the same place and same position as before. If it weren't for the different outfit, Lucy would've sworn he hadn't moved since they last met.

"Hello, Lucy," he greeted, "Nice to see you again."

"Nice to see you, too," she replied with a wide grin. She took her seat on the boulder. She was so happy to see him.

"What's up?"

"Not much. What about you?"

"Same. Anything happen yesterday?"

Lucy was about to reply with a no, but then she remembered what happened with Carolina.

She ended up telling Raphael all about the thing with the milk.

"She said no one cared about you?" Raphael replied when she finished, "What a load of crap."

"But she's right," Lucy answered, "No one really cares."

"I am offended," Raphael half-joked, "I'm someone."

"What?"

"I care about you. I have a feeling this isn't the first time something like this has happened to you."

"...No, it isn't. Carolina does stuff like this all the time. Well, not *exactly* like that. It's usually just spreading nasty rumors and getting me excluded from all the fun stuff at school."

"This 'Carolina,'" he said her name like it tasted bad, "sounds like a horrible person to me."

"I know, but what can I do about it? She's got everyone backing her and all I have is me."

"Once again, I am offended. I've got your back and I think you shouldn't let this Carolina walk all over you."

Lucy thought about it for a moment before she replied with conviction, "You know what? You're right! Why does she get to get away with being a monster? Why does she get to get away with dumping milk on my head?"

"She shouldn't."

Lucy stood up, "Why should I let her get away with throwing all the bad stuff in my face?! What makes that okay?!"

"Nothing."

Lucy turned to her friend, "I hate to leave so soon, but I just realized that there's something I need to do."

"I'll wait," he replied, as he began to strum a fast song on his guitar, "Tell me what happens."

"Will do," she replied as she began to jog off, filled with purpose.

Birds in the Rain

7

Lucy went to the grocery store on her way back to the home, just like she said she would. When Lucy returned to the home, she marched through the side door and placed the paper grocery sacks and her umbrella on the table and called out in her sing-song-iest voice.

"Carolina!" she sang as she fished through a brown paper sack, "Could you come here for a second?"

She didn't wait for Carolina to come to the kitchen. She waltzed forward and met her halfway. Blake turned on her usual stool, sipping her Coke. She even pulled off her headphones.

"What?" Carolina replied, barely paying attention.

Lucy beamed, "I felt bad for the milk thing, so I stopped by the grocery store and got some more milk. I just wanted to make sure I got the right kind this time." Lucy unscrewed the cap as Carolina examined it with a condescending smile.

"Yeah, it looks like you didn't screw up this time," Carolina replied, "Glad you learned your..." Before she could finish, Lucy poured the jug's contents onto her head.

Carolina held her mouth open in speechless shock as the milk soaked into her hair and designer clothes. It made her makeup mask run and made Lucy feel satisfied. Blake laughed.

"You're wrong, Carolina," Lucy growled as the skim milk ran out, "I care about what I think and feel. And I," Lucy paused as she thrust the jug into Carolina's petrified hands, "AM someone."

Before anyone could reply, Lucy turned and marched out the door, picking up her umbrella as she passed.

Later, Lucy recounted the whole thing to Raphael at the boulder.

"Ah! Justice!" he laughed. "How... cyclic."

"I never would've done that if not for you," Lucy replied honestly, "You gave me confidence."

"That was nothing. Just something people should do for each other, you know?"

Lucy chuckled, "Yeah, they should... Raphael, if any one treated me half as kindly as you do, then I'd be a completely different person."

Raphael stopped strumming on his guitar. He wore a confused smile on his face. He asked, "What makes you think that?"

"It's just..." Lucy blushed. For some reason the question made her embarrassed. "I... no one..."

"Lucy," Raphael cut off, much to Lucy's relief, "I know that people's words hurt. I know, trust me. But in the end, I realized that people's words shouldn't affect me *that much*. Let me save you the pain of having that epiphany on your own: you may never be as perfect as people want you to be. And maybe they already know that, but you're perfect enough just the way you are. The only person who should make you want to change is *yourself*."

Lucy stared at him, shocked. She couldn't speak, it felt wrong to move.

And Raphael just looked back, completely serious.

Then he just smiled. A tiny, reassuring smile.

And Lucy couldn't help it... she smiled back.

Then they started laughing hysterically, for absolutely no reason at all.

8

Lucy and Raphael spent the rest of the day talking, laughing, and making music. Raphael (obviously) was a very skilled musician. Lucy, however, had no idea that she possessed the talent for singing that she did. She had taken music classes before and the Sisters had taught her to sing in their choir, but she'd never possessed any passion for it.

Raphael had goaded her into singing along to a few chords and before Lucy knew what was happening, she was improvising song lyrics to Raphael's strumming.

Later that night, fresh out of the shower and wrapped in a towel, she wiped the steam off the mirror.

Then something magical happened.

Lucy had never thought of herself as beautiful, much less pretty. But that night, she looked at her face in the mirror and wondered what she'd been thinking all those years. She liked the way she looked. Her eyes were kaleidoscopes of shades of green and her skin was a pretty, pearly shade. She recalled memories of her flowing, black hair and thought of it as just that. Flowing, not thin or nappy or any of the other things Mrs. Dollar had told her.

But this realization didn't strike her because she was vain. Beauty have never meant much to her. It struck her because of the thought that seeped into her mind afterward.

If she had been wrong about her appearance, what else was she wrong about?

Her thoughts were cut off by an urgent rapping at the door.

"Lucy!" one of the younger girls' voice called, "Hurry up! I have to *pee!*"

Lucy hurried to get dressed and then stepped out of the bathroom.

She walked down the hall to the tower room and was about to pull the attic ladder down when a voice interrupted her.

"Hey! Lucy!"

Lucy gasped with surprise and turned to see Blake lounging on her bed. "Oh, Blake," Lucy replied, "I didn't see you there."

"What's been up with you lately?"

"What do you mean?"

"I may not know much about you, but I could've sworn yesterday I knew the difference between a sheep and... whatever you are now."

"Huh?"

Blake rolled her eyes as if she was saying the most straight-forward thing ever, "I wouldn't have pegged you as someone who would dump milk on Carolina's perfect little head."

"Well, I never really liked her."

"Pfft, no one does. She's a jerk."

Lucy laughed.

When the laughter ended it was replaced by an awkward silence.

Finally, surprising herself, Lucy replied, "I could say the same thing about you."

"What do you mean by that?"

"You never stick your neck out for anyone, at least not in my memory. Then, all of a sudden, you decided to help me yesterday? Why?"

Blake hesitated for a moment, tilting her head toward the ceiling. Then she answered, "Father Patrick's latest homily talked about treating others with kindness."

"Father? Homily?" Lucy parroted, "You're Catholic, too?"

Blake's eyes lit up with familiarity and joy. She leaned forward and replied, more enthusiastically than Lucy ever heard her say anything, "Yeah! I didn't know you were Catholic! This is great! I thought I was the only kid here!"

Lucy sat comfortably on the bed next to her and replied, "My first home was an abbey. I spent my first six years as a devout Catholic. I still go to church when I can and pray all the time, but I haven't been able to go to Mass since coming here. Mrs. Dollar won't let me."

Blake's eyes twinkled with mischief, "I sneak out every Saturday night to the Vigil Mass at St. Lucy's. I know where Mrs. Dollar keeps her car keys. I pack nice clothes in a duffle bag and then change in the bathroom at church. Wanna come this week?"

Lucy knew that Blake could drive. She served as Mrs. Dollar's chauffeur sometimes, driving her this way and that. "Yes," Lucy replied without hesitation.

9

"So now I have plans to sneak out and go to church with Blake," Lucy told Raphael the next day amidst the light shower of rain.

"That's kind of ironic, isn't it?" Raphael chuckled, "'Cause normal church-going kids don't sneak out and you and Blake are sneaking out to go to church."

"Hey! Why don't you come with us?" Lucy invited.

He faltered in his guitar-strumming. "No, I can't do that," he replied almost *too* quickly.

Lucy was confused, "Why not? I'm not gonna start preaching or anything, but everyone's always welcome in church."

"It's just," he seemed unnerved. "I...don't have any nice clothes. It would be rude of me to show up. Dressed like this." He was wearing the same outfit he'd worn the first day they'd met, leading Lucy to think he only owned two or three outfits.

"Okay..."

"Anyway," Raphael sought to change the subject, "you never told me your story." His calm, quiet strumming had resumed.

"That's because there isn't much to tell," Lucy replied with a shrug, "I never knew my parents. My mom dropped me off at a police station long before I could remember and I don't have any idea what my dad was doing right around then. The first six years of my life, I lived in an abbey and was raised as a devout Catholic by the Sisters. It was a pretty good life, all in all. I had all the moms and sisters I could ask for. I went to a catholic private school. I was full of faith and still am, really."

She continued, "then, when I was about six, the abbey burned down and I was removed from the home. I remember crying a lot and wondering if I'd ever see them again. Then I went through a string of foster homes and was always given back. Eventually they sent me here."

"Why?" Raphael inquired, "Why would they give you back?"

"I don't really know, actually. Up until recently, really recently, I thought it was my fault. That maybe I was doing something wrong. Now I realize that it was probably their issues, not mine."

"...You said that you were religious?"

"Well, not like crazy, hell-fire religious, if that's what you're thinking. I just think... no, I *know* that God's looking after me."

"...I admire your faith. Before the whole 'dying' thing, I kinda lost faith. I stopped going to church and stuff. One day, I just thought 'What does God care about me? He's never done a thing for me,' and just never thought of it again."

"Well, the way I see it, God's not the one who does bad things... it's people. And if he helped us all the time and did everything for us, then what would be the point in even living?"

Raphael looked at her for a moment before saying, "You know, you have a really good point there."

"Thank you."

Birds in the Rain

10

The next day, the skies were completely clear. Lucy and Blake spent most of the day in Lucy's room going over the plan of sneaking out.

They stuffed a duffle bag Blake owned with church-worthy clothes and shoes and then threw it into the back of Mrs. Dollar's van.

At about quarter-past ten, they snuck out of the kitchen side-door, wearing pajamas, as quietly as they could. Lucy barely dared to breath. In the sky, the moon was big and beautiful. Lucy knew it was a little ridiculous, but she liked to think that it was God's sign of approval.

Neither of the two girls dared to speak until they were about five miles away from the home.

"Phase one, complete," Blake chimed, miming a checkmark with her right hand.

"I've never done anything like this before," Lucy chuckled with excitement.

"My parents used to tell me stories of how they would get in all kinds of trouble for sneaking out."

"You remember your parents?" Lucy had only ever met a few kids in the foster system who'd actually known their parents and none who spoke as fondly of them as Blake did.

"Yeah, my parents were awesome. They were always supporting me and encouraging me to be myself and try new things. They were the best."

"What happened to them?" Lucy inquired in a squeaking voice.

Blake got a sad look in her eyes, "My mother was murdered. Her brother never liked my father, so he got my dad locked up for it. I know it wasn't my dad, though. My parents were lovesick for each other. They'd miss one another if they were apart for five seconds. The only thing they loved as much as each other was... well, me."

"Wow," Lucy replied, because she didn't know what else to say.

"And you know what really sucks?" Blake sounded angry now, "I actually know who killed my mom and no one believes me!"

"You do?!"

"Yeah, I watched from the closet as my stupid uncle killed her!"

"Oh my God..."

"He killed her so he could peg it on my dad and you know what else? Instead of taking me in like he was supposed to, he dumped me in the loony bin and left me in the system!"

"Why would he do that?"

"I don't know, something about a trust fund."

They were silent for a minute before Lucy spoke, "Well I believe you."

"That's why I wanna be a lawyer or a detective when I grow up. That way, I can get my uncle into and get my dad out of the joint."

Lucy didn't know what to say. She'd never really wanted anything as passionately as Blake wanted to free her father.

11

They pulled into the church parking lot just in time to change before the Mass started at eleven. They slipped into bathroom stalls and slid into their clothes.

Lucy was finished sooner. She was wearing a simple blue sweater-dress with short sleeves and stripy heels that were a little snug.

She inspected herself in the mirror before running her fingers through her hair.

Blake stepped out in front of the mirror. Lucy hardly recognized her.

Blake looked like someone out of a painting. Her ringlet curls framed her face with elegance and her smokey purple, floor-length dress was accented with black lace, giving it a victorian feel. Her blue eyes stood out like sapphires in a pile of coal.

Lucy didn't know what to say... again.

"What?" Blake asked, looking at her curiously.

"It's just..." Lucy stumbled, "You look... different."

"I know. I was never quite sure if I liked that feeling or not."

"What feeling?"

Blake turned and faced the mirror, "Being different from my normal self."

"Oh."

"Let's go get our seats."

The sanctuary was almost empty. Besides Lucy and Blake, there were only a handful of elderly women, a man in a wheelchair missing both his legs, and a college student that was pouring over her books even as she sat waiting for church to start.

Mass went by quickly. Lucy savored every moment. She especially loved Father Patrick's homily about family.

When church was over, Lucy and Blake changed back into their pajamas and drove back to the home.

"That felt great," Lucy yawned as they drove down the road, "but now I'm sleepy."

"I know," Blake replied, "but we'll be back at the home soon and we'll be able to get some rest."

"Say, Blake, does this mean we're friends?"

She seemed to think about it for a minute before replying, "Yeah, I guess it does. It's been awhile since I had a friend."

"I'm glad to hear that. That means I now have *two* friends."

"Two? Who's the first?"

"Oh, that would be Raphael."

"Who's that?"

"I met him a few days ago while I was on a walk. We talked a bit and we got along really well. I've seen him almost every day since."

"Is he the reason why you dumped milk on Carolina's head?"

"Well, he gave me the courage to do it. Does that count?"

"Yup. What's he like?"

"He's nice, calm... 'chill' would probably be a better way to describe him. He plays guitar a lot and I think he's a runaway."

"Why?"

"Just a few things... like what he told me of his past and how he only has two or three outfits. He always talks about his parents in the past tense."

"No, I mean, do you know why he ran away?"

"...No... I think it has something to do with his parents."

"Why do you think that?"

"He refers to them as things like 'my good-for-nothing parents' and stuff."

"Okay."

Birds in the Rain

12

Over the course of the next few months, Lucy continued to meet with Raphael and go to church with Blake. She learned a lot about her new friends.

Raphael not only played guitar, but the harmonica and the ukelele, which he taught her to use. He spoke three foreign languages fluently, Russian, German, and Spanish, all self-taught. He always had a Swiss Army knife nearby and he also liked black berries.

Blake had a diverse range of skills. Her father was a survival enthusiast and her mother had been a krav maga instructor (krav maga is a type of martial arts) and Blake had been both their star pupils. She kept a rosary and a bible, both of which had belonged to her mother, under her pillow. She dressed goth because she thought it made her look as tough as she was. Her favorite movie was *Casablanca* and she was a fan of a cool show called *Supernatural*, which was a show about brothers who fought demons and other monsters.

Lucy also learned a few things about herself. She learned she was a talented singer and a natural ukelele-player. She had a knack for picking up languages. She liked art by Claude Monet. She had opinions. She was pretty. She was a person.

She liked rain.

Raphael continued to help her discover herself and gain self-confidence.

Raphael, in some ways, made Lucy's life easier and harder all at once. On one hand, she could seed the good stuff now, She had hope again. Her life wasn't pointless. She wasn't pointless. On the other hand, now that she knew what she was worth, she realized that she didn't have to lay down and take all the crap she'd put up with for years. She found ways to fight the demons she now knew were not her fault. Some ways were subtle, but a lot were not. She snapped back at Mrs. Dollar and Carolina with witty remarks and out-shined them with logic.

People saw her now. People around town, people at school. They still assumed the worst, and sometimes they still spread rumors.

At first, the rumors hurt. Then she told Raphael about them and he just laughed. Between hysterics, he managed, "Those are so untrue! Is that *the best* they can come up with?" and just like that, they didn't hurt anymore. Plus, it didn't hurt that Blake beat up the guy who'd started the rumors.

Anyway, Raphael seemed to so easily fix everything about her that was broken. She could sit with him for hours, laughing, singing, talking, dreaming, escaping.

With him, she was free. She was no-holds-barred Lucy and no one else.

Things were happier, if not better. Then, one cloudy day, everything changed.

Blake and Lucy were walking home, talking about the future. They had been making plans to buy a car and work their way through college. They laughed after Lucy shuddered at the thought of a moldy apartment.

Suddenly, two guys stepped around a corner. One of them looked familiar to Lucy. She remembered him just moments before he spoke.

He pointed at them and exclaimed, "Them! Those two! They're the ones who got me beat up!"

"What?" Lucy replied, shocked that he'd dare mess with Blake again.

"Back off!" Blake exclaimed as she slid her back-pack off her shoulder and let it fall to the ground. The bigger guy stepped forward and cracked his knuckles.

"Make me," he bellowed. They stood looking at each other for a tense moment before the smaller guy lunged at Lucy. In an instant, both the guys were on the ground, the bigger guy squishing the younger guy under his weight, while Blake slammed her fists into his face.

She shouted, punctuated by the blows, "DON'T! TOUCH! MY! FRIEND!"

A police officer who'd been nearby ran over and dragged her off. His partner hand-cuffed the two guys while he hand-cuffed Blake.

"Hey!" Lucy shouted, "You can't do that! She was protecting me! She was defending herself!"

"Sorry kid," the officer answered insincerely.

"Look after my stuff for me," Blake said to Lucy as they shoved her in the car that had just pulled up.

"Blake!" Lucy shouted after her.

"Take care, Lucy!"

"Blake!" The next thing she knew. Lucy was standing alone on a street as two police cars drove away.

Birds in the Rain

13

The next few days wore on for Lucy.

After one day, Mrs. Dollar announced that Blake wasn't coming back to the home. Lucy managed to salvage Blake's most prized possessions before the other girls could take them.

Blake's favorite pair of combat boots, her mother's rosary, her father's Bible, the pocket watch with her last family photo glued inside, and her favorite leather jacket, the dress she wore to church, and the lipstick she wore with it were all stuffed in her duffle bag in the corner of Lucy's room.

After two days, Lucy went down to the local police station to see if she could find out what happened to Blake. All the police would tell her was that Blake was taken away, probably to be put in a new home.

After three days, Carolina started talking smack about Blake and Lucy lashed out, using every swear-word she knew in conjunction with a slap to Carolina's stupid face.

Carolina never spoke of Blake again.

After four days, Lucy didn't even leave her room. She wanted it to rain so she could talk to Raphael. She wanted Blake to come back.

After five days, she couldn't sleep. She began to hear the patter of rain on her skylight. She was beginning to wonder what Blake and Raphael were up to when she heard a distinctly non-rain tapping on her window.

She pushed out the skylight and looked outside. She didn't know what she had been expecting, but it definitely wasn't Raphael sitting on her roof.

More importantly, he looked hurt.

He smiled painfully and Lucy quickly ushered him inside.The light in the room was dim, relying only on the skylight for illumination. She reached to her dresser and found the lighter, then used in to light up the oil lamp.

When she turned to face Raphael, she nearly dropped the lighter in surprise.

Birds in the Rain

14

He had *wings.* Real, actual wings, that he nervously bunched up behind him.

Lucy wondered how she had never noticed before, then recalled where he always sat when they met. He could've easily hid his wings in those vines.

Lucy decided to swallow her questions and focus on what mattered most.

Raphael was hurt. He needed help.

She inspected the damage; gashes on his forehead, shards of glass imbedded in the wounds. His knuckles were a little scraped up, too. She opened the first-aid kit she kept under her bed and began to pick out the larger shards of glass with her fingers as she disinfected the wounds.

"How did this happen?" she questioned.

"The bloody wound on my head or... uh..." he flexed his wings in conclusion to the sentence and smiled nervously.

"The bloody head wound, of course!"

"Oh." It was clearly not the answer he was expecting, "I was walking down the street when this drunk guy came out of this bar and whacked me in the face with a bottle for no reason. I wiped the pavement with his face after that though."

"I figured."

There was an awkward silence. He winced every time she pulled glass from the cut or dabbed alcohol on the wound.

"So..." he finally said, "about the wings..."

"I don't care," Lucy interrupted, only realizing the truth of it as she said it, "I mean, I'm curious, but they really don't change anything."

There was another silence.

"...I didn't *always* have them. You know that little girl from the hospital I told you about? She... I guess she gave them to me..."

"How?"

"My last night in the hospital, she asked me, 'Do you ever wish you had wings?' Well, of course I did. She asked me what I'd do if I had them and I told her that I'd just fly away. She just nodded and left. That night, after I got back to my parent's apartment, I started to feel like crap. I went to my room and locked the door."

"For days," he continued, "I laid on my bed, trembling in pain. Intense pain. I felt like my insides were being ripped apart and mixed up. There was a deep ache in my bones... my blood felt like it was burning me from the inside out, and the pain was worst between my shoulder blades. I don't remember much, but I think the little girl from the hospital... I think she took care of me. Anyway, when I woke up, I felt different. I felt lighter, the air felt thicker, and... well, I looked and I had wings."

"Then you ran away?"

"Yep."

"You might need stitches."

"Really?" He swore. "Is there any way you can do it? I'd rather avoid hospitals."

"I can try, but I don't have anything to numb you up with."

"Ouch."

Another silence.

Lucy said, "They took Blake away."

"What?"

Lucy recounted what had happened the past few days.

Then there was another silence.

Lucy began again, "Do you think... that girl could give me wings, too?"

"...I'm pretty sure I could."

"How?"

"I don't know. I guess I just... do. Are you sure you want to, though? I mean, obviously there's no going back once it's done."

"I'm sure. Look around," she waved her arm around the room, "Now that Blake's gone, this is *everything* I have. I don't want to stay here and spend the rest of my life fighting demons."

He nodded slowly. "Fair enough. I told you how much it hurts, right?"

"Yeah."

"And you're *positive*?"

"Yes."

Another silence.

"I'll see you tomorrow, then, Lucy." He just left.

15

Lucy knew it was working when her whole body began seizing up with pain.

Raphael was right, it worst the worst physical pain imaginable. It was all-consuming. All she could do was curl up on her tiny bed and think, *It hurts. It hurts. It hurts.*

Raphael was there. He took care of her and, three days later, she woke up.

She felt lighter.

The air felt thicker.

She had wings.

Raphael smiled at her.

"Ready to fly?" he asked.

She smiled in reply and packed the few things she wanted to keep alongside Blake's in the duffle. She'd be sure to find her and give them back.The world suddenly seemed so full of possibility.

They climbed onto the roof, into a sun-shower.

Somehow, Lucy knew that she could fly just by flapping her powerful wings.

She held out her hand and caught the fat raindrops.

It was raining, the sun was shining, and it was beautiful.

Lucy laughed, "We're birds singing in the rain."

"We are, aren't we?" Raphael relied with a smile.

Then they were flying.

About The Author

Rachael Mockalis is a contributing author to the Storyshares library.

About The Publisher

Story Shares is a nonprofit focused on supporting the millions of teens and adults who struggle with reading by creating a new shelf in the library specifically for them. The ever-growing collection features content that is compelling and culturally relevant for teens and adults, yet still readable at a range of lower reading levels.

Story Shares generates content by engaging deeply with writers, bringing together a community to create this new kind of book. With more intriguing and approachable stories to choose from, the teens and adults who have fallen behind are improving their skills and beginning to discover the joy of reading. For more information, visit storyshares.org.

Easy to Read. Hard to Put Down.

Birds in the Rain